TYRONE
AND THE
SWAMP GANG

BY HANS WILHELM

Scholastic Inc.
New York   Toronto   London   Auckland   Sydney

ISBN 0-590-25474-X

12 11 10 9 8 7 6 5 4 3 2 1   5 6 7 8 9/9 0/0

Printed in the U.S.A.   09

First Scholastic printing, September 1995

To my father

It had been a bad year at school for Boland.
He was down to three friends —
Terry, Stego, and Stella.
They did not even have enough players
for a mean game of meteorite soccer.
Almost everybody else had joined the Swamp Gang.
The leader was Boland's worst enemy,
who was none other than...

TYRONE! Or Tyrone the Horrible, as he liked
to be called. Tyrone was the world's first bully,
and Boland was his favorite victim.

"Look—someone without a bandanna." Tyrone
laughed and grabbed hold of Boland. "Why
haven't you and your wimpy friends joined
the Swampies yet, you little shrimp?"

"Because we still have our brains!" said Boland.

"Oh yeah?" said Tyrone. "Well, remember that we've got ways to make you join. We're the greatest."

"Says who?" Boland asked.

"Says ME. And what I say goes!" Tyrone walked off with a nasty laugh.

"Maybe we should join the Swampies," Stego said. "Otherwise Tyrone will make our lives miserable."

"Join those morons?" cried Boland. "Are you nuts? We have better things to do than to follow that bully."

"Maybe he isn't so bad underneath," Stego said. "Maybe we could all become friends."

"Friends don't force others to do things they don't want to do," Boland pointed out.

"Don't you even like their cool bandannas?" Stella asked Boland. "Everybody is wearing them now."

"And the Swampies always look like they are having lots of fun," Terry added.

"What fun?" Boland said. "I only see them knuckling under to Tyrone."

One of the things Tyrone and his Swampies did for
fun was to play practical jokes. That night, for instance,
they poured tons of soap powder into the public fountain.

Before the sun came up, the joke had turned into a
big, messy, bubbly surprise for the whole neighborhood.

But the real surprise came when principal B.C. Scatterbone came to see the class the next morning. B.C. Scatterbone had rotten eyesight — but a perfect nose: He could smell a rat from a thousand dinosaur feet away.

"I trust that none of you reptilian angels is responsible for that mess," he said. He smiled a sickly smile that showed all his sharp yellow teeth.

"So," he continued, "I know you are all eager to clean up the fountain. I will personally supervise your efforts."

Everybody was stunned and angry — even the Swampies, although they tried hard to look cool and innocent.

The gang's morale was so low that Tyrone called an emergency meeting.

"We have to hit back!" he said. "And I know how!"

Tyrone told his plan to the gang.

"We'll give old Scatterbone's house a new coat of paint," he said. "That will make his eyes go gaga. But we've got to be quick and quiet and not get caught."

"Right on!" cried the Swampies.

Armed with paint and spray cans, they went to work — full blast.

But the real blast came the next morning. Once again, B.C. Scatterbone greeted the class.

"Thanks to some anonymous helpers, my house has received a new look during the night. Since I'm sure that none of you likes the colors or the designs, you will be only too happy to repaint my entire house from top to bottom."

"Rats!" said some of the kids. This was the second time they were getting blamed for something that they didn't do.

The Swampies grumbled loudest of all. Their joke had backfired again. "Maybe Tyrone's ideas aren't really so great," one whispered to another.

"Whatdoyoumean?" Tyrone cut in. "Somebody must have squealed on us. And I think I know who."

Boland couldn't believe he was in trouble again.
"I didn't squeal! I didn't squeal," he cried.

"How else did Scatterbone know it was us?" Tyrone demanded.

"I don't know," said Boland. "Maybe you just can't fool him. He can smell out anything."

"Okay," Tyrone said. "I'll let you off this time. Tonight we're going to fix old Scatterbone once and for all."

"What are you going to do?" Boland asked.

"None of your business. You stay out of it, you hear! Or else you can collect your bones at the Museum of Natural History!"

Boland was scared. . .

... but not *too* scared.

That night Boland spied on Tyrone and the Swampies.
He saw them dumping a large load of burning
lava rocks in front of B.C. Scatterbone's house.

Boland heard Tyrone whisper, "Hee hee. That will give old Scatterbone a hot surprise when he steps out tomorrow morning."

Boland ran for help as fast as he could. He got Stella, Terry, and Stego out of bed and told them what had happened.

Then he said, "Tyrone and his Swampies have gone crazy this time. This prank could really hurt somebody. Lava rocks are dangerous stuff. They could even burn the place down. We've got to work fast before Scatterbone wakes up."

The four friends carefully loaded all the
glowing rocks into the wheelbarrow.
They worked as quietly as possible.

Soon the danger was over.

"Let's clean up and leave no trace of the lava rocks,"
whispered Boland. "I can't wait to see Tyrone's
face in the morning when old Scatterbone comes
to school alive and well as usual."

"No need to wait till morning," said a sinister
voice behind him.

It was Tyrone!
"You lousy traitor," Tyrone growled and grabbed
Boland by the throat. "I'm going to get you for this."

"Wait, Tyrone!" Stella cried. "He was only trying to keep you from making a big mistake!"

"You keep out of this!" said Tyrone.

Suddenly they all heard a sharp click.

The door handle turned and the door creaked open.
Tyrone was so startled that he jumped straight up.

BOINK! He knocked his head against the branch of a tree.
In the next moment, he came crashing down...

right on top of the hot
and glowing lava rocks.

"ARRRUUUGH!"
He cried so loud that he
woke up the entire swamp
forest.

"AARRRUUGH!" he
cried again as he struggled
to his feet. Then he ran
away as fast as he could.
    This time his prank had
backfired in more ways
than one.

For several weeks after that Tyrone could
not sit down in class.

Suddenly all the bandannas disappeared.
The former Swampies were not eager to dress
like Tyrone anymore.

After all, Tyrone had to wear those
comfy little diapers until he was well again.
Who wanted to be like him now?